The
Christmas Croc
A Yuletide Fable

John P. Bourgeois

ISBN-10:069224932X
ISBN-13:9780692249321

The Christmas Croc

Listen now, Children! Hear that tick?
It tones for infants with colic,
and shitty tikes who always romp,
or sassy tweens with fucking pomp.

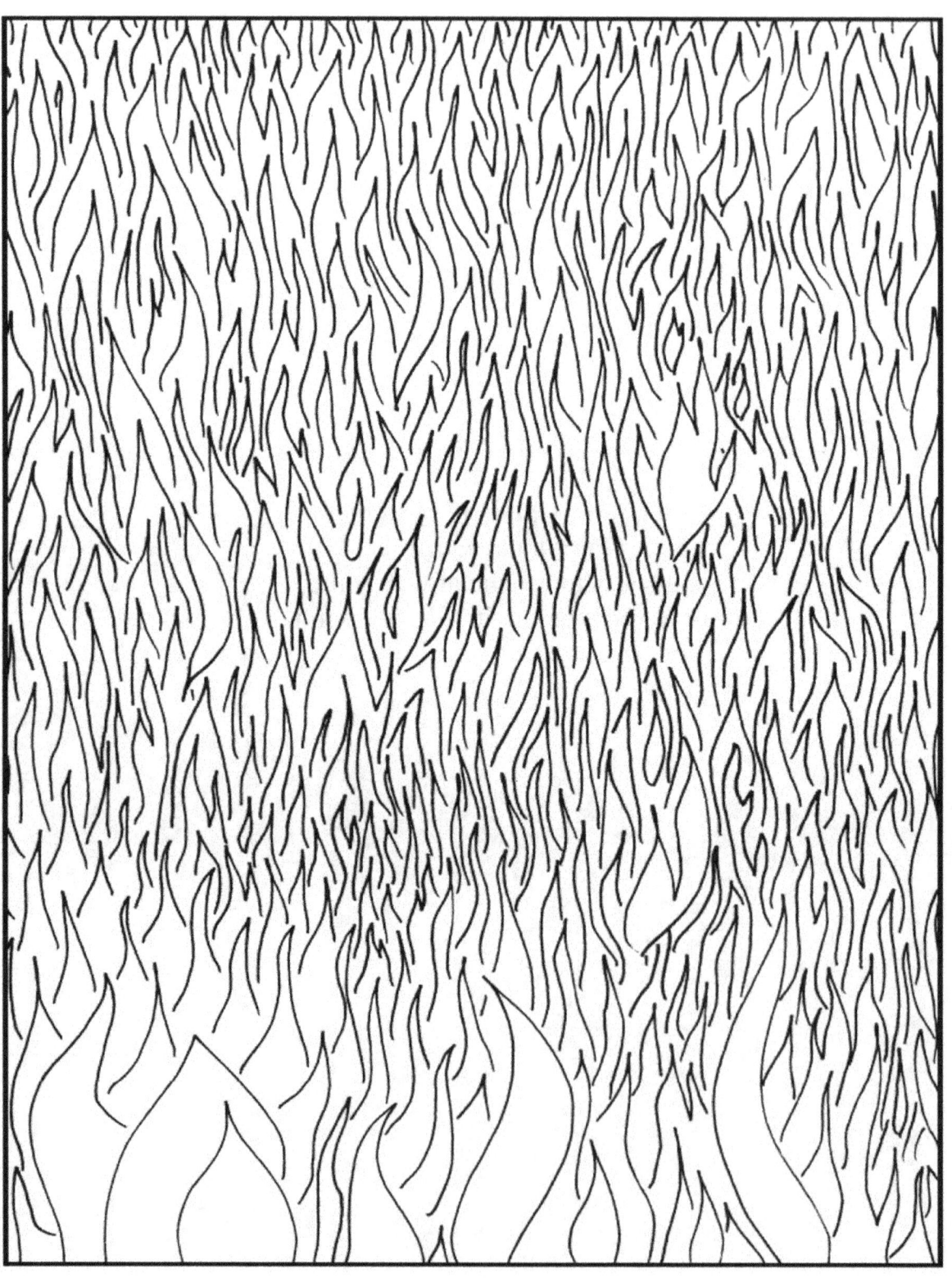

Father Christmas, or Père Noël,
sent a time beast straight from Hell.

Recall that croc from Neverland?
The one who ate the Captain's hand?
With Hook's right palm went down a clock
which causes that incessant tock..

Although it is a fierce reptile,
you need not fear the crocodile.

Santa sanctioned this great lizard
to munch bad kids in its gizzard.
But do not fret, Dears. You'll be fine,
just so long as you stay in line.

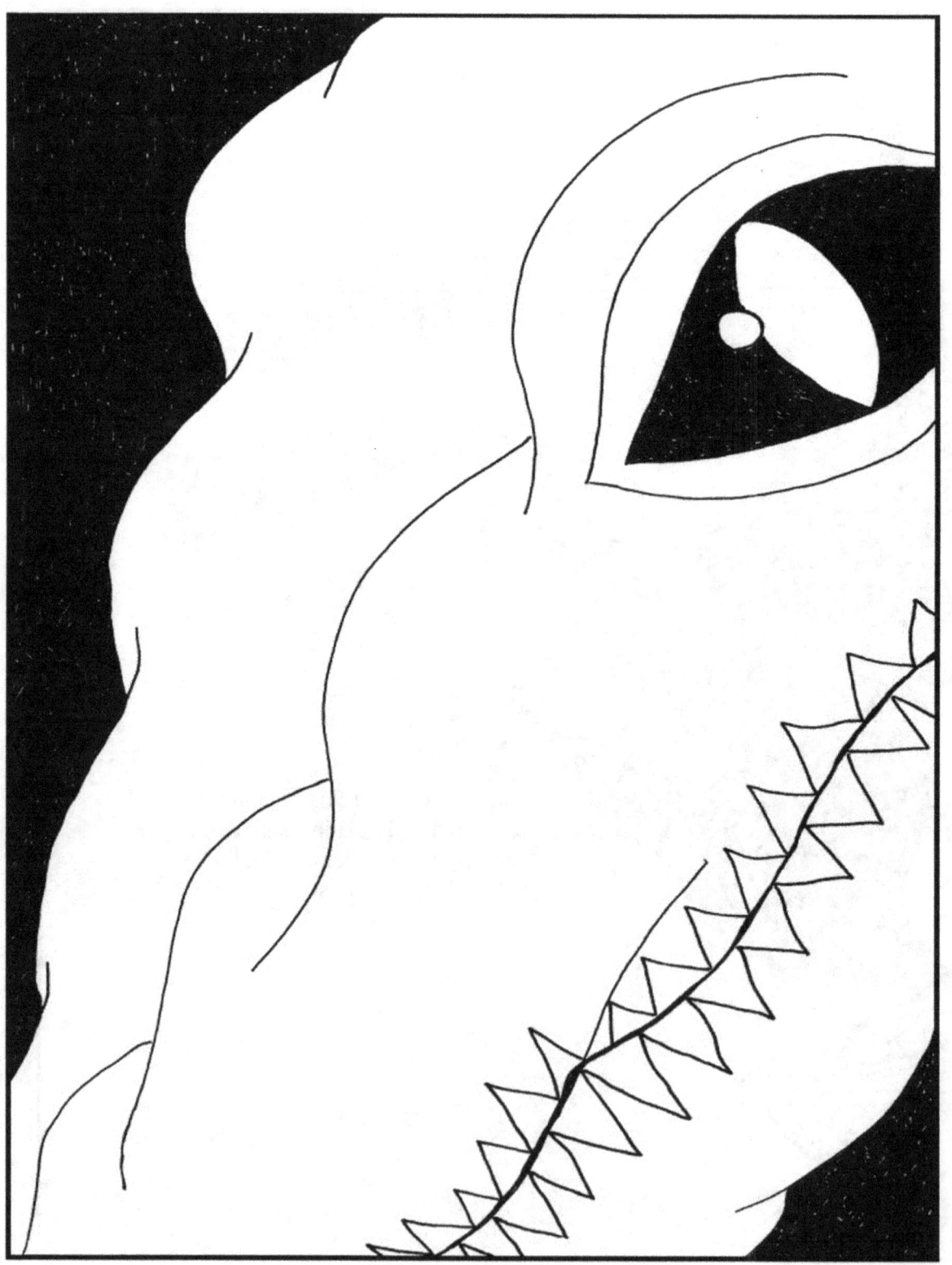

BUT! If you argue, lie, or fight,
the Christmas Croc comes in the night.

And in the morning, what is left
will be your bits it would not heft:
a blood-drenched mattress stained with goo
darkened flakes of sepia's hue.

Some bone debris; fragments of flesh;
flayed entrails that still smell fresh.

Your gory toys witness this feast
where you are ravaged by the beast.
The croc's long snout rips out your lungs
 and climbs your ribs like ladder rungs.

You'll remain conscious through it all.
The anguish hurts too much to bawl.

Atop the sheets, then by your side.
(You beg pardon from those belied.)
It slips its jaws around your head
and somersaults right off the bed.

When you're headless, it mounts your skull.
The scaly rhythm has a lull.

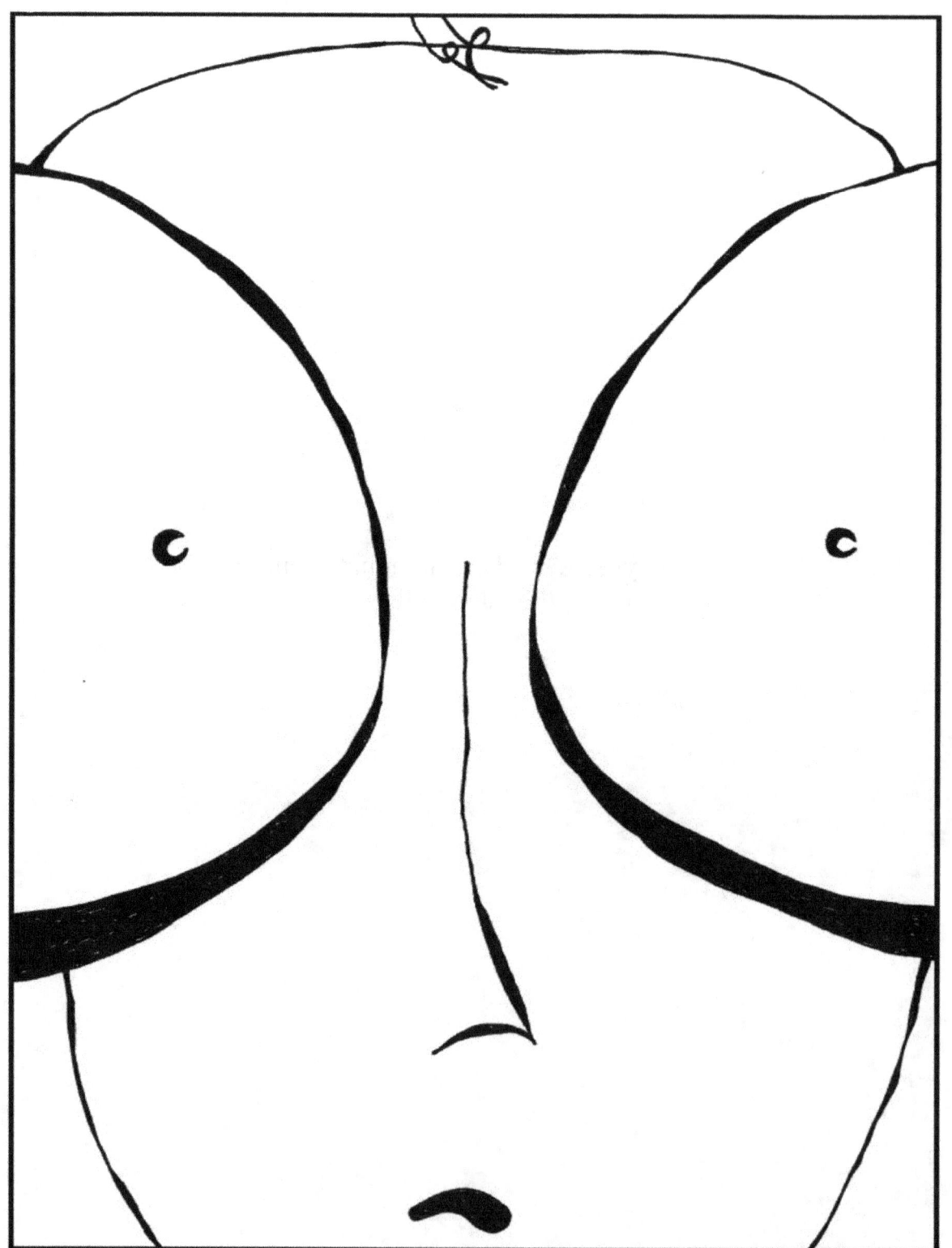

In the dark, you wake up screaming.
Were you just vividly dreaming?

Far off, distant, sharp flames lash
while echoing the magma's crash.

No longer in your room or home;
this is the croc's native roam.

Before you whisper a sole sound,
long-lobed elves stand all around,
 in shoes with bells and felted caps
 and faces lined like highway maps.

Off stone flooring you are hauled.
Mounds of clothes mark others mauled.

The processing elves quickly toil.
Your achy head begins to boil.
One elf notes your ears grow out.
You touch the point and damn near shout!

Bedazzled in green hosiery,
Teddy Line Three is where you'll be.

Hunched between two nameless drones,
carols screech over megaphones.

Thus across the factory floor,
naughty children slave evermore.

Got it, Darlings? You comprehend?
If your rooms you refuse to tend,...

The Christmas Croc will rape your corpse
and drudge your soul in doomed cohorts
that build gifts for good girls and boys.
Young occultists make better toys.

Now, shelve your childhoods far up high.
This concludes your last lullaby.

www.ingramcontent.com/pod-product-compliance
Lightning Source LLC
Chambersburg PA
CBHW081522050726
47503CB00018B/2952